This book belongs to

....

For Clare,
with thanks for the fifty years,
who loves Venice as much
as I do, and loves donkeys
almost as much.
M.M.

To Frieda,
on her first trip to Venice
H.S.

You can find out more about
Michael Morpurgo's books
by visiting his website at
www.michaelmorpurgo.com

EGMONT
We bring stories to life

Our story began over a century ago, when seventeen-year-old
Egmont Harald Petersen found a coin in the street.
He was on his way to buy a flyswatter, a small hand-operated
printing machine that he then set up in his tiny apartment.

The coin brought him such good luck that today Egmont
has offices in over 30 countries around the world.
And that lucky coin is still kept at the company's
head offices in Denmark.

First published in Great Britain 1995

This newly illustrated picture book edition
first published in Great Britain 2013
by Egmont UK Limited
The Yellow Building, 1 Nicholas Road, London W11 4AN
www.egmont.co.uk

Text copyright © Michael Morpurgo 1995
Illustrations copyright © Helen Stephens 2013
Michael Morpurgo and Helen Stephens have
asserted their moral rights.

ISBN 978 1 4052 6352 8 (Hardback)
ISBN 978 1 4052 6353 5 (Paperback)
ISBN 978 1 7803 1415 0 (Ebook)

A CIP catalogue record for this title is available
from The British Library.

Stay safe online. Any website addresses listed in this book are correct at the
time of going to print. However, Egmont is not responsible for content hosted
by third parties. Please be aware that online content can be subject to change
and websites can contain content that is unsuitable for children. We advise
that all children are supervised when using the internet.

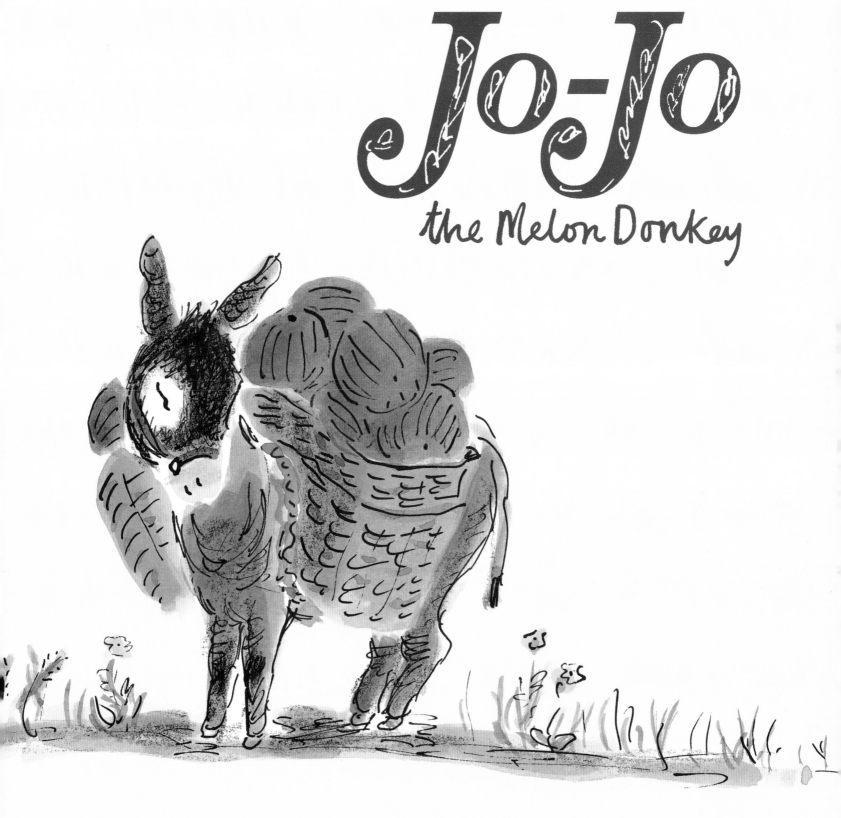

Jo-Jo

the Melon Donkey

Michael Morpurgo

Illustrated by Helen Stephens

EGMONT

J o-Jo was a donkey.
His father had been a donkey before him,
and his mother as well. Jo-Jo had to be a donkey
whether he liked it or not.

And he did not like it, not one bit.

Work began early for Jo-Jo.
First, his master would load
him with so many melons
that he could hardly walk.

Then he would lead him out of
the village and down the dusty road
towards the great city of Venice.

Jo-Jo loved Venice.

He loved the canals and the bridges
and the sound of the church bells
ringing out over the rooftops.

All day long his master would haul him
down the footpaths that ran alongside
the canals, and Jo-Jo would call out,
"Melons. Melons for sale!"

Everyone would know it was Jo-Jo
and come running with their money.
And all the while the flies came and
would not go away.

Only in the cool of the evening
resting under his olive tree,
were there no flies to bother him
and no master to bully him.
Then at last he could be at peace.

One misty sunrise his master woke him as usual.

"Up, up, you old ragbag," he shouted. "No more back streets for me. I've heard they'll pay double for melons in St Mark's Square. Even the Doge, the ruler of Venice himself, might buy one of my melons."

The load was even heavier that morning, but Jo-Jo didn't mind. He had a feeling inside him that something good was about to happen.

By the time they reached St Mark's Square
it was already full of people.

"Don't know why I never thought of this
before," said his master, unloading the
melons. "We'll sell them all in no time.
Sing out, you old ragbag you."

"Melons. Melons for sale!"
Jo-Jo brayed, and his cry rang around the square.

Everyone in St Mark's Square stopped and turned and looked.
And then one of them began to laugh, and then another and another
until the entire square was filled with laughter.

"What are you laughing at?" asked Jo-Jo's master.

"Above your head," they cried. Behind them stood the four golden
horses of Venice, the four most beautiful horses in all the world.
"Beauty and the beast!" roared the crowd.

Jo-Jo hung his head in shame.

All morning the people came to point and stare, but they bought no melons. Then, as noon chimed, the great doors of the Doge's Palace opened and a little girl ran out into the square, a nurse bustling after her.

"Come back, come back," the nurse cried.

"But I want a melon," said the little girl. "And anyway, I don't like being cooped up in that palace all day. I've got no friends to play with and I'm bored."

"It's the Doge's daughter," someone whispered; and soon everyone was there, bowing and curtseying as she passed. She ignored them all and made straight for the pile of melons beside Jo-Jo.

"How much do you want for one of your melons?"
she asked Jo-Jo's master.

"For Your Highness, it's a gift. I have the best
melons in all of Venice."

"Thank you," said the Doge's daughter.
Then she noticed Jo-Jo standing beside his master.
"He has such sad, kind eyes," she said. And she
reached out and stroked Jo-Jo on his neck.

Jo-Jo had never been patted in all his life,
and his knees weakened with joy.

"Really, Your Highness," said the nurse, "can't you see there are flies all over him? Come along back to the palace before your father sees you." And she hustled the little girl away.

Jo-Jo closed his eyes and held the picture of the little girl in his mind so that it would never go away.

Within a few minutes all the melons were sold. Anyone who was anyone in St Mark's Square was eating melons. What was good enough for the Doge's daughter was good enough for them.

So every day that summer, Jo-Jo came to St Mark's Square loaded
with melons and stood under the four golden horses in front of
the Cathedral. And every day the Doge's daughter came at noon
for her melon. She would always talk gently to him and smooth
his nose before she left.

One afternoon, Jo-Jo was gazing up
at the four shining golden horses,
as he often did.

"Oh, why can't I be like you?"
he cried.

His master woke from his snoring sleep.
"How dare you wake me like that?"
he roared. "No use talking to those
horses. Statues can't hear."

But Jo-Jo knew they could.

The very next morning, the Great Doge came
to the window of his palace.

Trumpets sounded and a crowd gathered.

"Be it known to one and all," said the Doge,
"that I intend to purchase the finest horse
in the city for my daughter's birthday. The
horse will be chosen at noon this very day!"

Jo-Jo stood and watched the
horses arriving in the square.
Every one of them was finer
than the one before and every
one made him feel smaller
and uglier than ever.

As the noon bell sounded,
the Great Doge came out into
the square with his daughter,
and the grand parade began.

"My daughter is ten years old today," he said,
"so she is quite old enough to choose for herself."
He turned to his daughter. "Now, my child, which
one would you like?"

The Doge's daughter walked slowly along the line,
and then at last she turned away and pointed.

"Over there!" she said, pointing towards
the four golden horses.

"You can't have the golden horses," said the Doge. "They belong to the people of Venice."

"Not them," the Doge's daughter said. "I want that one over there, the one that's standing by the melons, Father."

The crowd gasped.

"But that's a donkey!" the Doge cried.

"Yes, Father," said the Doge's daughter.

"I forbid it," said the Doge, "I absolutely forbid it. I cannot have a daughter of mine riding around on some flea-bitten donkey!"

"I don't want to ride around on him," said the Doge's daughter. "I want him to be my friend."

"Don't you argue with me," thundered the Doge. "You could have picked the finest horse in the land and you choose that walking carpet. Look at him with his feet curled up like Turkish slippers!"

"Father," said the Doge's daughter, her eyes filling with tears, "if I cannot have the donkey I don't want anything."

"All right," said the Doge. "If that's what you want then you will go without a present. Go back into the palace and go to your room at once."

But the Doge's daughter ran to where Jo-Jo stood and put her arms around his neck. "Come to the palace tonight," she whispered, "and wait outside my window. We shall run away together. Be there, Jo-Jo."

For the first time in his life, Jo-Jo was proud he was a donkey.

"Don't go getting any grand ideas inside that ugly head of yours,"
his master said. "You're just a donkey, and don't forget it.
Once a donkey, always a donkey. Do you hear me?"

Jo-Jo heard him, but he was not listening.

He was making plans.

In the black of the night Jo-Jo bit through the rope that tied him to his olive tree and made his way carefully back into Venice. It was a wild, wet and windy night. No one heard Jo-Jo hurrying through the empty streets, trotting over the little bridges, towards the Doge's Palace.

And then he heard the voices. At first he thought it must have
been the wind whistling through the towers and spires of the city.
But then he looked up. The four golden horses spoke as one.

"Little donkey, little donkey," they said. "Listen to us, little donkey.
The sea is coming in. You must wake the people and warn them.
Tell them to leave. They will drown if you do not save them.
Hurry, little donkey, hurry!"

Jo-Jo galloped across the square until he reached the water's edge. He could hear the waves rolling in towards him from the sea. He felt the water washing over his hooves and saw it running down over the stones and into the square behind him. He lifted his head, took the deepest breath of his life, and then he brayed and he brayed until his head ached with it.

The Doge's daughter was waiting for Jo-Jo.

"Not so loud, Jo-Jo," she said. "You'll wake everyone up."

And then she too heard the distant roar of the sea and heard
the waves rolling in. She felt the water round her ankles
and understood why Jo-Jo was braying.
She knew at once what had to be done.

With the Doge's daughter on his back, Jo-Jo trotted
braying through the city streets, waking everyone up.

"What?" they shouted, opening their windows.
"Melons at this time of night?"

"No, no!" cried the Doge's daughter.
"The sea has broken in and the city is under water!"

And all the while the sea came in,
flooding the square and the Cathedral
and the Doge's Palace itself.
Woken by Jo-Jo's braying, the people
of Venice ran for their lives.

Jo-Jo the melon donkey, with the
Doge's daughter on his back, guided
the children and the old people to
safety down the flooding streets.

And all the time the waters rose round them.
Houses crumbled and the great bell tower in
the square came crashing down into the water.

When morning came they discovered that not a single life had been lost. Jo-Jo, the melon donkey, had saved the people of Venice, and they loved him for it.

It was the people who asked the Doge to put up a statue, a golden statue of the melon donkey. It should stand, they said, in St Mark's Square in front of the golden horses themselves, so that no one should ever forget him.

At the unveiling ceremony the Doge placed a laurel on Jo-Jo's head and apologised for the cruel things he had said about him.

"There is a legend," the Doge said, "that if ever the people of Venice were in danger, the four golden horses would save them. It's a nice story, but it's just a story. It was Jo-Jo the melon donkey who saved us and we must never forget it."

And Jo-Jo smiled secretly inside himself and was happy.

Never again was Jo-Jo made to carry anything: except, that is,
for the garlands of flowers that people put around his neck whenever
he went out for a walk. For he became the Doge's daughter's donkey.
And he was her friend and constant companion for the rest of his life.

And donkeys do live for
donkey's years, you know.

I remember standing in St Mark's Square, when I first went to Venice — a while ago now — and gazing up in wonder at the four golden horses of Venice on St Mark's Cathedral. They were to me the most beautiful sculptures I'd ever seen — over a thousand years old.

Behind me was the famous Campanile, the great bell tower of Venice, which I knew had collapsed only a century or so before — I'd seen an amazing photograph of it actually in the process of falling down.

And there too was the Doge's Palace, where the Doges of Venice always lived, and I thought that maybe one of these Doges had a daughter, and one day she sees a donkey in the square, a melon donkey. Everyone laughs at him, his master beats him. This donkey longs to be loved, longs to be as beautiful and as admired as the golden horses up there on the Cathedral. And the Doge's daughter sees him standing there and loves him at once, tells him how beautiful he is, and so he loves her too.

Then add to all this the fact that my wife Clare adores donkeys. I decided to write a donkey story for her, and set it in Venice. That's how Jo-Jo the Melon Donkey became a story.

Michael Morpurgo